For Mink, Mink Daddy, Sarah and their beloved companions.
- I. Cori Baill

For Alex, Dakota, Sandra, and C.H. for all their love and support.
- Heather Bell

Published by River Grove Books
Austin, TX
www.rivergrovebooks.com

Distributed by River Grove Books

Design and composition by Greenleaf Book Group and Heather Bell
Cover design by Heather Bell
Illustrations by Heather Bell
Art in Max's room by Dakota Wilson and landscapes throughout house by Sandra Bell

Publisher's Cataloging-in-Publication data is available.

Print ISBN: 978-1-63299-377-9
eBook ISBN: 978-1-63299-378-6

First Edition

Why is Mommy Crying?

—explaining early pregnancy loss
to young children

Written by I. Cori Baill, MD
Illustrated by Heather Bell

"I woke up," said Max.

Max wasn't afraid of the dark.

"Should we knock on Mommy and Daddy's door?"
Max asked Mink.

"Mommy will say, 'Come in!'
Dad will say, 'Does the little bird want
to be in the nest?'"

It was always warm between Mommy and Daddy.

"Look Mink," Max said.
"Mommy's not in her bed."

"Is Mommy crying?"
Max asked Mink.

"Mommy?" asked Max.
"Do you have an owwie? I get you a Band-Aid!"

"No son, I don't need a Band-Aid," Mommy said.
"It's not that kind of owwie."

"What are you two buddies doing up?" Mommy asked. "If you're cold in your jammies, you can rock with me."

Max liked how he fit under
Mommy's chin.

"How'd you get an owwie?"
asked Max.

"Do you remember what Daddy and I told you
about how babies come to people that love one another?" Mommy asked.

"Oh, I know that!" Max said. "Babies come from God."

"That is why you are so special," Mommy whispered to Max.

"I know that, too!"

"Sometimes," Mommy told Max, "a baby only starts on its way to their family."

"Sometimes a baby returns to be with God."

"Is that what happened to our baby?"
asked Max.

"Yes," Mommy answered.

"Did it hurt?" asked Max.

"Not much," Mommy answered. "But it made me sad."

"Mommy?" asked Max.

"Yes?" Mommy answered.

"Me too."

"Mommy?" asked Max.

"Yes?" Mommy answered.

"When that happens and the baby doesn't come, does the mommy have to go back too?" Max felt sick.

"Does she have to go take care of the baby?" Max asked.

"Oh, NO!" Mommy said. "I'm here with you. I won't leave."

Mommy hugged Max and Mink.

"God will take care of our baby.
He almost never needs a mommy, too."

"That's good Mommy," Max said.

He felt better.

"Mommy?" asked Max.

"Yes?" Mommy answered.

"Do you think God has arms?" Max asked.

Mom shook her head. "I don't know."

"I do!" Max said.

"You do?" Mommy asked.

"Oh yes Mommy, I know!"
Max said.
"That is how he picks up the babies to
give to mommies and daddies."

"I think you might be right,"
Mommy answered.

"I'm glad you and Daddy got picked for me," Max said.
"Me too," Mommy answered.

But Max was already asleep.

Max yelled, "Good morning! Time to get up!"

"Come in!" Mommy answered.

"Does the little bird want to be in the nest?" asked Daddy.

Max found his favorite place.

It was nice and warm.

Additional Resources

- National Alliance for Grieving Children- Locate Regional Support
  https://childrengrieve.org/find-support

- American Academy of Pediatrics: HealthyChildren.org,
  Responding to Children's Emotional Needs During Times of Crisis

  English:

  https://www.healthychildren.org/English/healthy-living/
  emotional-wellness/Pages/Responding-to-Childrens-
  Emotional-Needs-During-Times-of-Crisis.aspx

  Spanish:

  https://www.healthychildren.org/spanish/healthy-living/
  emotional-wellness/paginas/responding-to-childrens-
  emotional-needs-during-times-of-crisis.aspx

- Compassionate Friends (100+ languages available):
  https://www.compassionatefriends.org/grief/

- Star Legacy Foundation: https://www.starlegacyfoundation.org

CPSIA information can be obtained
at www.ICGtesting.com
Printed in the USA
BVRC100354140421
604812BV00016BA/368